HALLOWEEN
GOOD NIGHT

REBECCA GRABILL

ILLUSTRATED BY ELLA OKSTAD

ATHENEUM BOOKS FOR YOUNG READERS
NEW YORK   LONDON   TORONTO   SYDNEY   NEW DELHI

ATHENEUM BOOKS FOR YOUNG READERS

An imprint of Simon & Schuster Children's Publishing Division

1230 Avenue of the Americas, New York, New York 10020

Text copyright © 2017 by Rebecca Grabill

Illustrations copyright © 2017 by Ella Okstad

For information about special discounts for bulk purchases, please contact Simon & Schuster Special Sales at 1-866-506-1949 or business@simonandschuster.com.

The Simon & Schuster Speakers Bureau can bring authors to your live event. For more information or to book an event, contact the Simon & Schuster Speakers Bureau at 1-866-248-3049 or visit our website at www.simonspeakers.com.

Book design by Sonia Chaghatzbanian

The text for this book was set in Itchy Handwriting.

The illustrations for this book were rendered digitally.

Manufactured in China

0517 SCP

First Edition

2 4 6 8 10 9 7 5 3 1

Library of Congress Cataloging-in-Publication Data

Names: Grabill, Rebecca, author. | Okstad, Ella K., illustrator.

Title: Halloween good night / Rebecca Grabill ; illustrated by Ella Okstad.

Description: First edition. | New York : Atheneum Books For Young Readers, [2017]

Summary: "Ghastly ghouls count down to Halloween"— Provided by publisher.

Identifiers: LCCN 2015045509

ISBN 978-1-4814-5061-4

ISBN 978-1-4814-5062-1 (eBook)

Subjects: | CYAC: Stories in rhyme. | Halloween—Fiction.

Classification: LCC PZ8.3.G7214 Hal 2017 | DDC [E]—dc23

LC record available at http://lccn.loc.gov/2015045509

To Nicholas
$(y - \sqrt{|x|})^2 + x^2 = 4$
—R. G.

Lurking in the swampland,
lanterns glowing like the sun,
sits a massive mama globster
with her bitty globby one.
"Ooze," drools the mama.
"We'll slooze!" drips the one.
So they squish and they slosh
through the muck toward the fun.

Deep within the forest,
under ferns slick with dew,
flits a wee father wood imp
with his tiny implings two.
"Taunt," cackles Imp Dad.
"We'll fool," giggle two.
So they plot silly tricks
as a treat just for you.

Gliding through the moonlight
to a lone willow tree
are a watchful mother werewolf
and her wild wolflings three.

"Race," howls the mother.
"We'll chase!" yowl the three.
So they bound through the grass—
Going where? You will see!

Silent in the silo,
on a dry, dusty floor,
lies a wrapped mommy mummy
with her bandaged babies four.
"Rise," moans the mummy.
"We're dressed," rasp the four.
So they shuffle and they shimmy
out the old, creaky door.

Yonder in the boneyard,
where the bats swoop and dive,
breathes an old granny zombie
with her peeling zomblings five.

"Walk!" seethes the granny.
"We'll waltz," wheeze the five
as they lurch through the streets
crying, "Ghouls, come alive!"

High above the playground
on their brittle broomsticks
swoop a cloaked mama witchy
and her warty witchies six.

"Curse," orders Mama.
"We'll hex!" screech the six
as they soar over town
casting spells none can fix.

On a deli's Dumpster
crying, "Oh, this is heaven!"
perches Granddaddy Goblin
with his gnarly goblins seven.
"Dive," hollers Granddad.
"Bacon!" yell the seven.
Then they crawl down the street
as the clock chimes eleven.

Drifting toward your party
while the ghouls fill their plates
are a vague mother phantom
and her ghastly ghosties eight.
"Knock, knock," whispers Mother.
"Boooo!" wail the eight,
and they sail through your door
as the hour stretches late.

Upstairs in your hallway,
where the sun cannot shine,
lingers pale Papa Vampire
with his blood-drinking nine.
"Seek," trills Pa Vampire.
"We'll find," purr the nine
as they glide down the hall.
"Yes, now we will dine!"

Waiting in your closet
for your bedtime once again,
sits a grown daddy boggart
with his beastly boggies ten.
"Come," says Sir Boggart.
"We're here," cheer the ten,
and they sing, "We will get you,
and you'll never know when!"

"What?" screech ten wee boggarts.
"You're awake?" cry vampires nine.
"But we wanted to scare you,"
the eight ghosties whine.

"Drink?" wail seven goblins.
"Game?" ask witches six.
"Story?" beg five zombies.
"About the river Styx?"

"My loves, you know it's bedtime,"
you tell your ghoulish friends
and lead them toward the boneyard,
past the deli, round the bend.

Hug those four small mummies
and sleepy werewolves three,

kiss two drowsy wood imps,

pull one globster from a tree.

"Sleep now, morning's coming,"
you tell your monsters sweet,
so they snuggle into bed
and murmur, "Trick or treat!"